CÉZANNE'S PARROT

BY AMY GUGLIELMO

ILLUSTRATED BY BRETT HELQUIST

putnam

G. P. Putnam's Sons

In the French countryside, near blooming lavender fields, in a little yellow house lived an artist named Paul Cézanne and his new parrot, Bisou.

"Bonjour, Bisou!" Cézanne said as he fed the bird a grape.

"Can you say, 'Cézanne is a great painter'?" he asked, hoping someday someone would tell him it was true.

But the bird just plucked at his feathers and said nothing.

For years, Cézanne had struggled as an artist in Paris. While other artists painted portraits of aristocrats and grand scenes from history and mythology, Cézanne depicted ordinary people and everyday places. While other artists painted flawless details with tiny brushes and delicate strokes, Cézanne preferred thick paint and heavy marks.

So when Cézanne submitted his portfolio to the famous Académie des Beaux-Arts, where the most talented students from around the world studied, the professors scoffed.

Cézanne fumed, "My hair is longer than my talent."

But his friend Monet offered some advice:

"Go to the country and paint what you see."

And so, Cézanne packed his supplies and journeyed south with Bisou, determined to become a truly great painter.

With a fresh canvas in hand, Cézanne wandered through fragrant
meadows until he found the perfect view of trees stretching toward the sun.

While Monet could paint quickly,
finishing a painting in a single day,
Cézanne was painstakingly slow.

For many weeks, he toiled away on the same canvas, carefully choosing each dab of pigment and measuring each brushstroke. It took over one hundred visits to his special hilltop to finish that one scene.

And every evening upon his return, the artist presented the parrot with his latest work.

"Repeat after me," he said as he passed the bird a plum. "'Cézanne is a great painter!'"

Bisou opened his beak as if to speak . . .

But he just yawned instead.

For months, Cézanne labored over just a few paintings.
Some took years to complete, some remained unfinished,
and some were hurled into the fire.

After much consideration, Cézanne chose his best pieces
and returned to Paris to apply to the Salon, the official
art show of the Académie.

When Cézanne toured the school, he thought all the students' work looked the same. Everyone was imitating the famous artists who came before them.

But Cézanne didn't care about tradition. He didn't want to follow the rules. He wanted to do something new.

The professors balked when they reviewed his submissions.

Cézanne was devastated. "I lack the magnificent richness of color that animates nature," he complained. "Use brighter colors," his friend Pissarro suggested.

And so, Cézanne returned to the country with his parrot, eager to make his paintings come alive with color.

He convinced a friend to be his model and instructed him not to move.
When the man sneezed, Cézanne had a fit.
"Sit still," he said. "Be an apple!"
The man posed for hours until the sun disappeared and he snored
in his chair.
He sat for a single portrait over one hundred fifty times,
until one day he didn't come back.

And each night, after a long day's work, the artist danced toward Bisou's perch to present his progress.

"Say 'Cézanne is a great painter!'" he begged as he handed Bisou a fig.

But the vibrant parrot only fluffed his feathered chest and coughed.

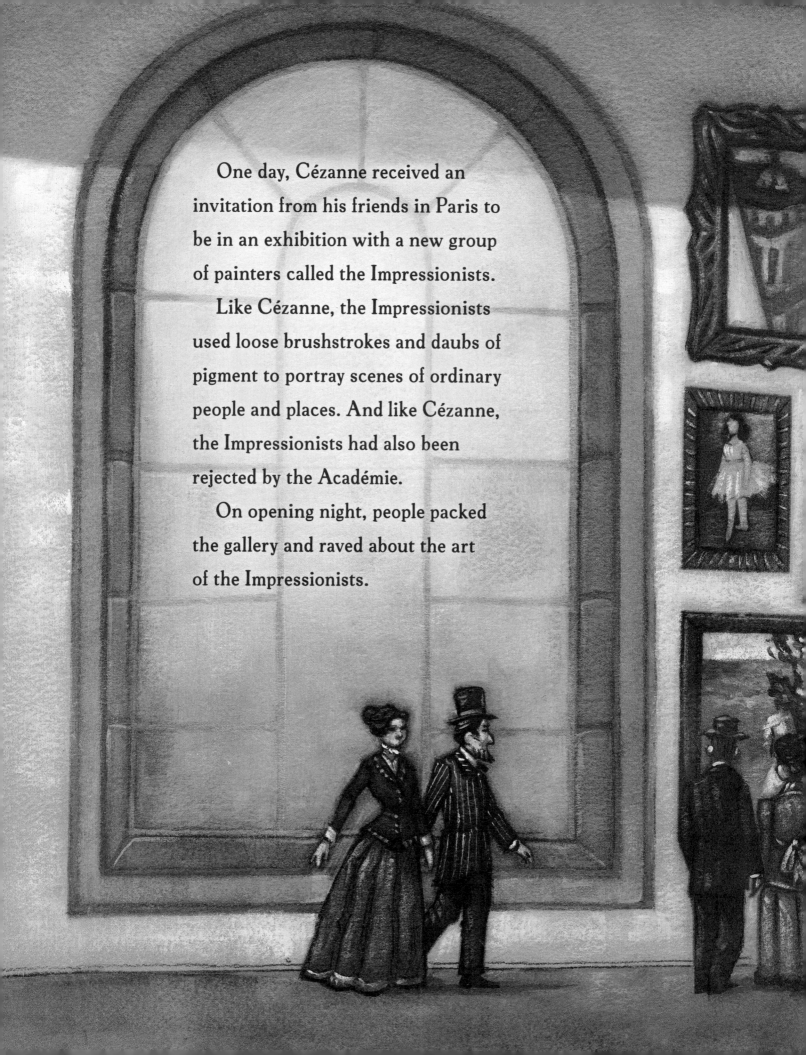

One day, Cézanne received an invitation from his friends in Paris to be in an exhibition with a new group of painters called the Impressionists.

Like Cézanne, the Impressionists used loose brushstrokes and daubs of pigment to portray scenes of ordinary people and places. And like Cézanne, the Impressionists had also been rejected by the Académie.

On opening night, people packed the gallery and raved about the art of the Impressionists.

Still, Cézanne's work was different. His friends wanted to capture the color and light of a single moment in time. But Cézanne didn't care about painting things exactly how they looked. Even among a group of rebels, Cézanne did not fit in. When the crowd noticed Cézanne's unusual style, they roared with laughter.

Cézanne poked holes in his canvases and broke his brushes.

Luckily, his friend Renoir saved a small watercolor.

"How does he do it?" Renoir marveled.

Monet agreed, but Cézanne snapped,
"You, too, are making fun of me!"

When Cézanne returned home,
he decided he would ignore the critics and paint what
he wanted, how he wanted. He knew people might laugh or say his style
was ugly. After all, he was painting in a way no one else had done before.

Cézanne set out a vase of flowers and dipped his brush into the vivid
pigments on his palette. But he worked so slowly that,
after days of toiling, the flowers drooped
and lost their petals.

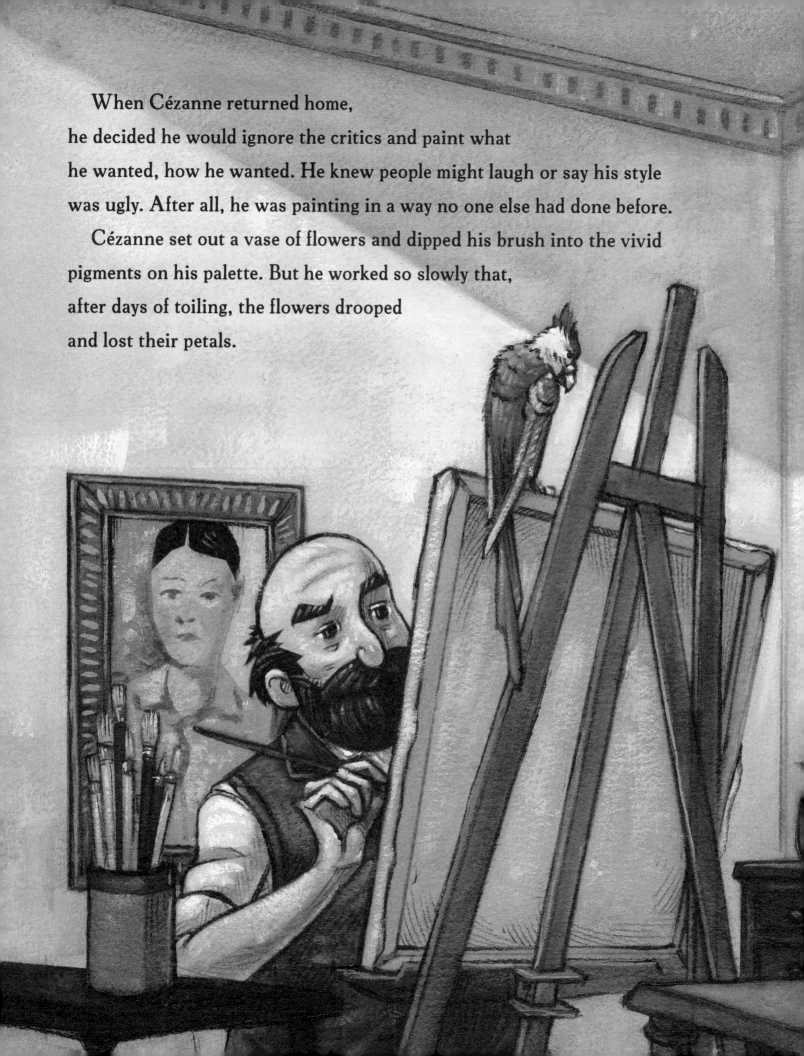

One morning, before Cézanne could say hello,
Bisou greeted him with a squawk.

BONJOUR!

"Now say 'Cézanne is a great painter!'" the artist said
excitedly as he fed the bird a peach.

But Bisou just blinked.

Cézanne groaned and arranged a napkin and a dish
of fruit on his studio table.

The artist worked tirelessly,
days into nights, only taking
breaks to eat and sleep.

Then one day, as Cézanne stepped back to admire
his finished work, his friend Gauguin dropped in to
see his recent pieces.

When Cézanne revealed the fresh still life, he heard
a commotion coming from Bisou's cage.

Cézanne opened the door to hand Bisou a pear,
but the lively parrot flew from the cage . . .

. . . and landed on the easel.

Bisou whistled, his carmine plumes standing up like a crown.

CÉZANNE IS A GREAT PAINTER!

Gauguin agreed.
He loved the painting
so much, he bought it!

The artist laughed and handed Bisou an apple. Then he scattered the remaining fruit across the table.

"Aha!" exclaimed Cézanne as he envisioned a masterpiece. The artist dabbed scarlet onto a fresh canvas. He scraped, slashed, and slapped at the paint with a knife, smiling.

"I will astonish Paris with an apple!" he declared.

And he did.

CÉZANNE IS A GREAT PAINTER!

AUTHOR'S NOTE

The artist Paul Cézanne really did have a pet parrot that he taught to say, "Cézanne is a great painter!" Why would he do such a thing? He probably needed the encouragement. Although he painted his entire life, Cézanne struggled for recognition throughout his long career, achieving success only toward the end of his life.

Born in Aix-en-Provence, France, in 1839, Cézanne developed artistic aspirations at a young age. In the 1860s, he moved to Paris—a city filled with literary and artistic activity—to study painting. He applied to the Académie des Beaux-Arts in 1861 but was denied entry. Subsequently, the Salon, the official art exhibition of the Académie, rejected Cézanne's submissions every year from 1864 to 1869.

While in Paris, Cézanne was highly influenced by a group of painters called the Impressionists, including his mentor, artist Camille Pissarro. Pissarro encouraged Cézanne to paint outside—*en plein air*—like other young artists of the time, rather than sitting in a studio. And so, after years of rejection from collectors and critics in Paris, Cézanne moved to the French countryside to paint in solitude.

In 1874, Cézanne returned to Paris to participate in the *Première Exposition* of the Impressionist artists. His work was badly received by critics and the public, so he skipped the second exhibition. He did submit to the third exhibition in 1877, but once again his work was panned. Cézanne didn't feel his style meshed with the Impressionists, so he parted ways with his friends. Indeed, historians now describe Cézanne as a Post-Impressionist, indicating that his work belongs to a subsequent movement of artistic inquiry.

Unlike his contemporaries, who focused on landscapes, Cézanne turned his interest toward the still life genre of painting, focusing on arrangements of fruit, flowers, and everyday objects. Cézanne spent so much time on each painting that the fruit would spoil, so he would have to use wax models. He really did say, "I will astonish Paris with an apple," and today he is best known for his still lifes of fruit.

Eventually, in 1895, at the age of fifty-six, Cézanne gained interest from a gallery in Paris that agreed to show 150 of his canvases, including several still lifes of apples. The show was a smashing success. Every last painting sold, even when they raised the prices! The exhibition was such a sensation, the gallery owner traveled to the countryside in 1899 and bought everything in Cézanne's studio.

What changed? Throughout his life, Cézanne experimented with his technique with varying success, and over the years, his style evolved and matured. Finally, at the end of the nineteenth century, that experimentation paid off, and his innovation and contribution to art was recognized and celebrated. His work was seen as fresh and modern, and young painters traveled to Aix-en-Provence to seek his guidance.

Cézanne was so obsessed with his work, he often stopped only to eat, sleep, and attend church. He even missed his own mother's funeral in order to paint. For portraits, he famously made his models pose for hours at a time, sometimes for over 150 sessions. Cézanne pledged to paint until the day he died. And he did: In 1906, he caught pneumonia when he was painting outside in a storm and died three days later.

Today, Cézanne's paintings are considered masterpieces and are some of the most expensive works of art ever sold. Cézanne is now known as the father of modern art, and his work has influenced many other famous painters like Paul Gauguin, Pablo Picasso, and Henri Matisse. Picasso, considered by many to be the greatest artist of the twentieth century, said, "My one and only master . . . Cézanne was like the father of us all."

SELECTED BIBLIOGRAPHY

While most of the research for *Cézanne's Parrot* was gathered from the sources listed below, I was fortunate to spend time with some of the paintings mentioned in this story at the following museums: the Metropolitan Museum of Art, New York; the Art Institute of Chicago, Chicago; the Musée d'Orsay, Paris; the Solomon R. Guggenheim Museum, New York; the Museum of Modern Art, New York; and the Whitney Museum of American Art, New York.

Danchev, Alex. *Cézanne: A Life.* New York: Pantheon, 2012.

Duranty, Edmond. *Le Pays Des Arts.* Paris: Charpentier, 1881.

Kendall, Richard. *Cézanne by Himself.* London: Time Warner, 2004.

Rewald, John, ed. *Paul Cézanne: Letters.* Boston: Da Capo Press, 1995.

Trachtman, Paul. "Cézanne: The Man Who Changed the Landscape of Art." *Smithsonian*, January 1, 2006, 82–88.

Vollard, Ambroise. *Cézanne.* New York: Dover, 1984.

SOURCE NOTES

The story of Cézanne's parrot was first written about in 1881 by the French art critic and novelist Edmond Duranty. In his book *Le Pays Des Arts*, Duranty recounts a visit to Cézanne's studio: "The parrot's voice rang out, 'He is a great painter.' 'He's my art critic,' the painter told me with a disturbing grin" [p. 317].

In *Cézanne's Parrot*, the dialogue between Cézanne and his parrot was re-created and invented by the author. Also, several lines of dialogue have been invented to illustrate the reception of Cézanne's work at the time.

Other quotes in the story were gathered from the following sources: "My hair is longer than . . ." Trachtman [p. 85]; "I lack the magnificent . . ." Rewald [p. 327]; "Be an apple!" Trachtman [p.85]; "How does he do it?" Trachtman [p. 86]; "You, too, are making fun . . ." Trachtman [p. 86]; "I will astonish Paris . . ." Trachtman [p. 82].

THE PAINTINGS BY PAUL CÉZANNE IN THIS BOOK

pg. 6: *Portrait of a Young Man*, 1866, Private Collection

pg. 10–11: *The Clearing*, 1867, Private Collection

pg. 19–21: *Portrait of Victor Chocquet, Seated*, 1877, Columbus Museum of Art, Columbus, OH, USA

pg. 24: *Crossroads of the Rue Rémy, Auvers*, 1872, Musée d'Orsay, Paris, France

pg. 26: *Portrait of Madame Cézanne*, c. 1885–1890, Musée d'Orsay, Paris, France (once owned by Henri Matisse)

pg. 32–33: *Still Life with Fruit Dish*, c. 1879–1880, Museum of Modern Art, New York, NY, USA

pg. 36: *Fruit and Jug on a Table*, c. 1890–1894, Museum of Fine Arts, Boston, MA, USA (once owned by Paul Gauguin)

pg. 37: *Still Life with Apples and a Pot of Primroses*, c. 1890, The Metropolitan Museum of Art, New York, NY, USA (once owned by Claude Monet)

For Brian G., parrot whisperer—A.G.

For Robert Barrett, who taught me how to paint—B.H.

G. P. PUTNAM'S SONS

an imprint of Penguin Random House LLC, New York

Visit us online at penguinrandomhouse.com

Library of Congress Cataloging-in-Publication Data

Names: Guglielmo, Amy, author. | Helquist, Brett, illustrator.

Title: Cézanne's parrot / by Amy Guglielmo ; illustrated by Brett Helquist.

Description: New York, NY : G. P. Putnam's Sons, [2020]

Summary: Paul Cézanne longs to be a great painter, but even with the advice of his friends Monet and Pissarro,

no one, not even his parrot, is impressed with his work.

Identifiers: LCCN 2017037138 | ISBN 9780525515081 (hc) | ISBN 9780525515098 (epub fixed) | ISBN 9780525515111 (kf8/kindle) |

Subjects: LCSH: Cézanne, Paul, 1839-1906—Juvenile fiction. | CYAC: Cézanne, Paul, 1839-1906—Fiction. | Artists—Fiction. |

Painting, French—Fiction. | Parrots—Fiction. | France—History—19th century—Fiction.

Classification: LCC PZ7.1.G84 Ce 2020 | DDC [Fic]—dc23

LC record available at https://lccn.loc.gov/2017037138

Manufactured in China by RR Donnelley Asia Printing Solutions Ltd.

ISBN 9780525515081

1 3 5 7 9 10 8 6 4 2

Design by Marikka Tamura.

Text set in Cooper Old Style URW.

The art was done in oil on paper.